For
Megan Lily Cowling

First U.S. edition 2007

Library of Congress Cataloging-in-Publication Data is available.

Library of Congress Catalog Card Number 2006933848

ISBN 978-0-7636-3461-2

2 4 6 8 10 9 7 5 3 1

Printed in Thailand

This book was typeset in Cochin.
The illustrations were done in acrylic and watercolor.

Candlewick Press
2067 Massachusetts Avenue
Cambridge, Massachusetts 02140

visit us at www.candlewick.com

CANDLEWICK PRESS
CAMBRIDGE, MASSACHUSETTS

# THE OLD TREE

## Ruth Brown

EARLY ONE MORNING, Pigeon Post was delivering the mail to the Old Tree.

"Hello, Mrs. Rabbit. Lots of cards for you today. By the way, did you know there's a big X painted on your tree? What's it for?"

"No idea," replied Mrs. Rabbit. "I'm *far* too busy with the new baby. My seventeenth she is, and as quiet as a mouse, thank goodness. Grumpy old Mr. Badger always moans about my kids, but those parakeets make more noise than all of mine put together. They should find a home and settle down like the rest of us."

# BANG~BANG, BANG~BANG.

"Who's there?" growled Mr. Badger.

"Only the post," called Pigeon. "I've got a package for you. It's probably those slippers you ordered."

**"HHHMMMPH,"** grunted Mr. Badger. "I thought you were the Rabbit kids banging their ball against my door. And as for those parakeets . . . Frightened to go out, I am."

"Well," said Pigeon, "if you do go out, you'll see a big X painted on your tree. Do you know what it's for?"

"No," barked Mr. Badger, and he slammed the door.

# DING-DONG, DING-DONG.

"Morning, Mr. Squirrel."

"Morning, Pigeon!" shouted Mr. Squirrel. There was a deafening noise above. "That woodpecker upstairs is driving me *nuts* with his renovations!"

"Have you seen the big X on the tree?" shouted Pigeon. "Who did it?"

"Don't know," bawled Mr. Squirrel. "But I bet my boys will be blamed. It's far more likely to be those parakeets . . . always hanging around and screeching."

Next, Pigeon stopped outside Mr. Woodpecker's door, but it was pointless to knock. He was making far too much noise sawing and hammering, so she slipped his home improvement magazine through his mail slot.

# TING~A~LING, TING~A~LING.

"Good morning, Professor Owl. How are you today?"

"Dreadful," moaned the professor. "I've got an *appalling* headache because of the screeching of those frightful parakeets, not to mention that remodeling fanatic downstairs."

"So you haven't been outside then?" asked Pigeon. "You haven't seen the X on your tree? I was hoping you would know what it means."

"Outside? Outside?" said Professor Owl with a shudder. "The sun is *far* too bright for my eyes. Good day to you, madam."

"Hello, *darling*," said Maggie Magpie before Pigeon even had a chance to ring the bell. "What's the gossip today then? Are those parakeets still driving everyone crazy?"

Pigeon laughed. "Today's mail looks official. Have you been thieving again, Maggie?"

"It's not *thieving*, darling. It's what magpies *do*. We see shiny, sparkly things and we pick them up. I suppose all those busybodies downstairs think I'm a thief?"

"I don't know," replied Pigeon. "But I do know that you've got a big X on your tree."

"Really, *darling*?" said Maggie. "Is it shiny?"

Next, Pigeon made her way to the very top of the tree.

# DONG~ALONG, DONG~ALONG.

"Ahoy there, shipmate," called Captain Crow. "Welcome aboard!"

"Postcard," was all that the breathless pigeon could say. "And"—*puff, puff*—"a big X"—*puff, puff*—"on your tree. What does it mean?"

Captain Crow was busy reading his postcard. But seconds later, he realized what Pigeon had said. "X? Did you say an X on our tree? Shiver me timbers! I know what an X means, matey!" But Pigeon had already gone. Captain Crow looked through his telescope, and his worst fears were confirmed.

E veryone except Mr. Woodpecker was outside staring up at the huge X.
What could it mean?
Who could have done it?
And *why*?
Suddenly they heard

## DONG~ALONG, DONG~ALONG.

Captain Crow was frantically ringing his bell and pointing. But no one understood him— he was too far away.

So for the first time ever, Captain Crow went down to the bottom of the tree.

"The X," gasped Captain Crow. "I *know* what it means . . . saw through my telescope . . . woodsmen . . . sawing down trees . . . with Xs on them . . . like ours. . . . They're going to cut down our tree!"

"What shall we do?" shrieked the animals. Then everyone froze.

CHOP, CHOP, CHOP. . . .

Sawdust started to rain down on them. Bits of bark flew through the air. Chunks of wood thudded around them.

They were *terrified*. "HELP, HELP!" they screamed. "Our tree! Our home! Don't chop it down!"

Then the chopping noise stopped. But the pandemonium didn't. . . .

"BE QUIET!" shouted Pigeon, but nobody heard. She took out her whistle and blew it long and loud. Everyone quieted down, even the parakeets.

Then a small cough broke the silence. They all looked up. The X was gone! Instead there was a hole — and in it, a very dusty Mr. Woodpecker!

He coughed again. "I need a bit more space," he explained, "so I'm building an addition. Do you think you could give me a hand?"

Since Mr. Woodpecker had given them such a fright, everyone started to shout at him, but Pigeon stopped them.

"Listen . . . LISTEN! I've got an idea that *might* save your tree."

"*Captain Crow*—go back up top and keep watch. *Squirrels*—you're strong; go help Mr. Woodpecker. *Professor Owl*—you check the measurements. *Maggie*—you're artistic; start painting. *Mr. Badger*—keep the little ones amused. *Mrs. Rabbit*—make us all a nice cup of tea. And finally, you parakeets, *please keep quiet.*"

For the first time *ever,* they worked together. It took the whole day, but by the evening, all traces of the X were gone and Mr. Woodpecker's new addition was in place. In fact, it looked as if it had always been there.

Everyone was *very* pleased and *very* tired. They all slept soundly that night—except the parakeets.

The next morning, everyone woke to hear voices outside . . . human voices. They all listened, hoping that, for once, those pesky parakeets would keep quiet, too.

"Well, look at that. I could have *sworn* we painted an X on this tree. But there's only an old birdhouse here—and look what's in it!" said the voice.

"Gosh," said the other voice. "Looks rather special, eh? Better not touch it." And the two woodsmen walked away.

DONG, DONG, DONG!
Captain Crow rang his bell.

Everyone rushed out into the sunshine, sure now that their tree was safe.

"Three cheers for Mr. Woodpecker," they cried.

"No, no," protested Mr. Woodpecker. "Our new neighbors are the ones who saved our tree."

"What new neighbors?" they asked.

"US!" called the parakeets as they popped out of the house — one . . . two . . . and a new baby—three!

"HIP, HIP, HOORAY!" everyone cheered. And that night they had a wonderful party.